The Jaguar and the Javelin

by A.H. Benjamin and Yuliya Somina

W
FRANKLIN WATTS

Franklin Watts
First published in Great Britain in 2016 by The Watts Publishing Group

ISBN 978 1 4451 4547 1 (hbk)
ISBN 978 1 4451 4549 5 (pbk)
ISBN 978 1 4451 4548 8 (library ebook)

Series Editor: Melanie Palmer
Series Advisor: Catherine Glavina
Series Designer: Peter Scoulding

Printed in China

Franklin Watts
An imprint of
Hachette Children's Group
Part of The Watts Publishing Group
Carmelite House
50 Victoria Embankment
London EC4Y 0DZ

An Hachette UK Company
www.hachette.co.uk

www.franklinwatts.co.uk

Jaguar was good at sports. He had won lots of Olympic medals.

That's because Jaguar was fast ...

strong ...

agile ...

brave ...

... and so graceful!

Jaguar won medals at every sport. Except ...

... at the javelin. Jaguar couldn't get the hang of it ...

no matter how hard

he tried!

The javelin always flew the wrong way.

“Watch out!” cried the judges.

Jaguar was sure it was the javelin's fault.

“I’ll make my own,”
he said.

So he did. The first javelin flew to the right.

“Argh!” shrieked Parrot.

The second javelin went left instead.

"Be careful!" shouted Monkey.

Jaguar didn't see as he threw his javelins about.

They went everywhere!

Jaguar gave up.

He sat down.

“Javelins don’t like me,”

he said, sadly.

Just then ...

"Help!" cried a voice.

It was Snake who had got himself tied into a knot.

Jaguar soon untied him.

"Thank you," said Snake.
"Is there anything I can
do for you?"

"Er ... yes!" cried Jaguar.
"You look just right!"

He told Snake his idea.

A few days later, Jaguar won a gold medal. Snake was the perfect javelin!

Puzzle 1

Put these pictures in the correct order.
Now tell the story in your own words.
How short can you make the story?